Freckleface Strawberry

and the

Dodgeball Bully

Freckleface Strawberry

and the
Dodgeball Bully

Julianne Moore

illustrated by LeUyen Pham

SCHOLASTIC INC.
New York Toronto London Auckland
Sydney Mexico City New Delhi Hong Kong

ISBN 978-0-545-24102-1

12 11 10 9 8 7 6 5 4   10 11 12 13 14 15/0

Printed in the U.S.A.   40

First Scholastic printing, February 2010

Typeset in Bodoni Six Book and Minya Nouvelle
Illustrations rendered with a Japanese brush pen and digitally colored
Book design by Donna Mark

For Bart, who loves to play ball

—J. M.

To little Maya Bee

—L. P.

Freckleface Strawberry goes to school.
Her mom and dad go to work.
Sometimes they have to go to work early.

That means Freckleface Strawberry
can go to Early Bird.

At Early Bird, kids get to play BEFORE
school starts. It means you don't have to be
at home eating extra breakfast.

Extra PLAY, not extra breakfast.

Freckleface Strawberry's dad drops
her off at the playground.

She plays four square and
jump rope—good.

She plays tetherball—okay.

She plays imaginary
monster ruling
the solar system—
EXCELLENT.

She plays anything she wants to,
unless it's raining. Because
when it rains, there is only . . .

DODGEBALL.

Scary dodgeball.

Hairy dodgeball.

Very, VERY
DODGEBALL.

Freckleface Strawberry does not like dodgeball. She does not like dodgeball because it is too fast and it is too hard. But mostly she does not like dodgeball because of Windy Pants Patrick.

Windy Pants Patrick is big.
Windy Pants Patrick is fast.
Windy Pants Patrick throws
the ball TOO HARD!

When a kid gets hit
by the ball, they are out.
It sounds like it hurts.

The sound is like:

And sometimes like:

But mostly like:

One rainy day, Freckleface Strawberry
came up with a plan.

She would stay in the back and practice her monster.

She would hop on her feet all the way in the back.

She would look like she was playing, but no one would know!

Windy Pants Patrick
threw the first ball.

Down went a kid
in the front.

THUNK!

Out went two girls
holding hands.

EEEK!

AAARGHHH!

Somebody's hat
flew off.

Freckleface Strawberry practiced her monster.

Windy Pants Patrick
threw one more ball.

BOP!

Freckleface Strawberry
hopped on one foot.

Windy Pants Patrick
hit the ball
with his head.

Freckleface Strawberry
sang a monster song.

Windy Pants Patrick yelled,
"Who's the last kid?"

Freckleface Strawberry looked up from her game.

All the other kids were out.

All the other kids were GONE.

Freckleface Strawberry was the last kid.

She got ready to scream. She got ready to cry.
Freckleface Strawberry just knew it was
going to hurt, hurt, HURT!

And then . . .

You're OUT! I WIN! Out, out, out! Game over! I win!

What? Did the ball get me out?

And the funny thing was,
she didn't really notice it.

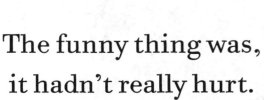

The funny thing was,
it hadn't really hurt.

The funny thing was,
she wasn't really scared.

ROAR!

I'm a monster, and I don't care!

Freckleface Strawberry said,
"I'm just pretending.
I'm not really a monster."

And Windy Pants
Patrick said, "Okay."

Just then the bell rang. It was time
to go into the classroom.

The next day was a sunny day,
and Early Bird was back out on the
playground. Freckleface Strawberry
and Windy Pants Patrick played
jungle gym monkeys.

And NOBODY got scared.